Leighton, Jessica and Jeannette,

Make this story your own. Savor those fleeting "little" moments together. Remember the snuggles.

♡ Jackie

After reading this story, come back and draw tiny pictures of things you find special. You could tuck little things here, too. Or write messages… It's up to you.

Each time you come back to the story, look at your pictures and remember your love as it grows. This is your story, too.

Meow Meow Meow

JACKIE BENNER
ILLUSTRATIONS BY KATHY ADLER

Text Copyright 2024 by Jackie Benner. Illustrations by Kathy Adler. All rights reserved.

This story is dedicated to my two. It is the story of how my love for them has grown, changed, and deepened during our time together.

   Eric and Morgan (Baby Cat) Benner,
      Both of you are woven into this story.
      I love you beyond the moon
      and on into eternity.
      How blessed I am that you were sent into my life.
      I love each stage of us.
      I am Your Lucky Momma.
                  Love, YLMomma

Momma Cat felt that the day Baby Cat was born was the most beautiful day there ever was.

She snuggled her Baby Cat close to her, and purred happily.

As she looked at her sleeping baby, she hoped she would be a good and loving Momma Cat to this sweet little one.

Momma Cat promised Baby Cat that she would be the best momma she could for Baby Cat.

As she made that promise, she whispered to her sleeping kitten…

Meow meow meow.

And so, they began their lives together.

Momma Cat took good care of Baby Cat when she was very little.

Momma Cat would
     feed her,
     bathe her,
     show her new things,
     meow kitty songs with her,
     and chase the rainbows across the floor with her.

When they were tired they would have a snuggle and rest.

And at the end of each busy day, when Momma Cat tucked Baby Cat into her kit-ten bed she would softy whisper…

Meow meow meow.

When Baby Cat got a bit older, she and Momma Cat would go on Adventures together!

They would find the mythical mice hiding in the house and chase them away.

They would go out into the big, big yard and find things that flew and tiny things that crept silently in the grass.

They would have a snuggle and nap in the shade of a lazy azalea bush.

And, sometimes, on beautiful warm days, they would lay in the warm grass, look at the cloud shapes in the sky and Momma Cat would whisper…

Meow meow meow.

In time, Baby Cat began to show Momma Cat the things she had found. Momma Cat was amazed by a beautiful tiny flower she would never have seen if not for the keen eyes of Baby Cat.

Momma Cat smiled at the sparkly, roll-y bead Baby Cat found under the couch.

There was a rainbow on the floor made by the crystal hanging in the sun-shiny window. Baby Cat rolled the bead into the rainbow and the two began a game of batting the bead back and forth, back and forth to one another through all the cheerful colors.

Each day, Baby Cat found exciting new things to share with Momma Cat. They were magical things Momma Cat would never have seen if not for Baby Cat.

And at night, after a full day of Adventuring, Momma Cat would tuck Baby Cat into her kit-ten bed and whisper…

Meow meow meow.

Time passed.

Sometimes now Baby Cat went off on her own Adventures.

Momma Cat missed her kit-ten but couldn't wait to hear about all the things her Baby Cat had seen and done.

And Baby Cat grew.

Baby Cat grew into a grown up cat herself.

Still, sometimes she and Momma Cat sat side by side and saw how beautiful the world was…

especially when they sat side by side.

Momma Cat would tell her Baby Cat about all the things she, too, had done while they were apart.

But, each knew they were in the heart of the other even when they were not together.

On each reunion, the two felt such contentment when they sat, warm fur to warm fur, and were just... Momma Cat and Baby Cat.

And Momma Cat would whisper...

***Meow meow meow.*ъ**

As they sat that way

– together –

-Momma Cat and Baby Cat-

Baby Cat whispered back…

I love you, too.

**Not the end.
It is endless…**

About the Author

Jackie Benner is a retired elementary school teacher from Howard County, Maryland. She taught grades 3 - 5 as a classroom teacher and K-5 as a Gifted & Talented Program Specialist. After she retired, she worked K - 12 as a substitute teacher. She loved it all!

Jackie lives with her husband and two pups, Nellie Donuts, the Rescue Mix, and Dottie the Spotted Dachshund. Jackie did have cats when she was growing up and was claimed by an amazing and wonderful gray cat named Nipper. He lives forever in her heart. Sadly, everyone in her family is allergic to cats so there are no kit-tens (other than grown up Morgan) in her home now.

Jackie has two grownup children, Eric and Morgan, who are the Lights of her Life. How blessed can one mom get?

Jackie loves reading, working with her church family, visiting with loved ones, camping, music, planting flowers, the beach, and living in the happiness of now.

Jackie is very thankful for the talented, giving, funny, intelligent, creative people with whom she finds herself surrounded… wonderful friends. indeed! (For example: Kathy Adler, with whom she was so fortunate to work at an elementary school in Maryland!) .

*M*eow meow meow is Jackie's first book and she is very thankful for the encouragement and support of so many people who believed in her.

"You should write a book,"
they said…

Here it is!

About the Illustrator

Kathy Adler is a retired third grade teaching assistant. She and author Jackie Benner worked together in the same elementary school in Maryland. Little did they think, when doing recess duty, that they would be collaborating their talents on a book.

Kathy and her husband live in Highland, Maryland. She is lucky to have her two grown sons and one little grandson living nearby. She spends summers in her Durango, Colorado home with many visiting friends and family.

Kathy enjoys hiking, photographing memories of her travels, babysitting her grandson, reading, attending the theater, painting and drawing, and creating handmade art books that include her paintings and poetry. Watercolors and acrylics are her favorite painting mediums, and landscapes and florals are her preferred subjects. She loves painting "her mountain" in southwest Colorado and the surrounding flora and fauna. But she enjoys all forms of artistic creation; pottery, sewing, art journaling, carpentry, paper folding, collage, sculpture, writing poetry and building rock cairns by a river. Often a hand-made card turns into a book, or a pile of sticks turns into a horse sculpture.

Thanks to Jackie Benner, these are Kathy's first, officially published book illustrations.

With Thanks:

Bruce, Eric, Morgan, Kathy Adler, Terri Via, Louise Wall, Lisa Trovillion, Marla Stahl, and Danny Adler (Kathy's son and Jackie's former student).

MANY thanks for patiently helping guide me and offering encouragement as this book came into being.

I thank, as well, the many, many others who helped get me through the rough times of my life.

My heart is full with the blessings of you all.

Meow meow meow.

More pages for little drawings and tucked in things!

The original:
"Meow meow meow."
"Meow meow meow, meow."

Made in the USA
Middletown, DE
18 July 2024

57611436R00020